Period(s) Covered In This Journal

____

TopicPage(s)

NOTES

NOTES

NOTES

NOTES

NOTES

NOTES

NOTES

NOTES

NOTES

N
O
T
E
S

NOTES

N
O
T
E
S

NOTES